COOL CLASSICS

CAMARO

CHEVY'S FAST FRIEND

BY JAY SCHLEIFER

Crestwood House
New York

Maxwell Macmillan Canada
Toronto

Maxwell Macmillan International
New York   Oxford   Singapore   Sydney

Crestwood House
Macmillan Publishing Company
866 Third Avenue
New York, NY 10022

Maxwell Macmillan Canada, Inc.
1200 Eglinton Avenue East
Suite 200
Don Mills, Ontario M3C 3N1

Macmillan Publishing Company is part of the Maxwell Communication
Group of Companies.

First edition

Produced by Twelfth House Productions

Designed by R studio T

Photographs by Jeff Greenberg

Printed in the United States of America

10 9 8 7 6 5 4 3 2 1

Library of Congress Cataloging-in-Publication Data

Schleifer, Jay.
Camaro / by Jay Schleifer. — 1st ed.
p.   cm.—(Cool classics)
Summary: Discusses the history of the Camaro automobile, initially
introduced as Chevrolet's rival to Ford's Mustang but which went on
to become a classic car in its own right.
ISBN 0-89686-696-3
1. Camaro automobile—Juvenile literature.   [1. Camaro automobile.]
I. Title.   II. Series.
TL215.C33S35   1993
629.222'2—dc20   92-3809

CONTENTS

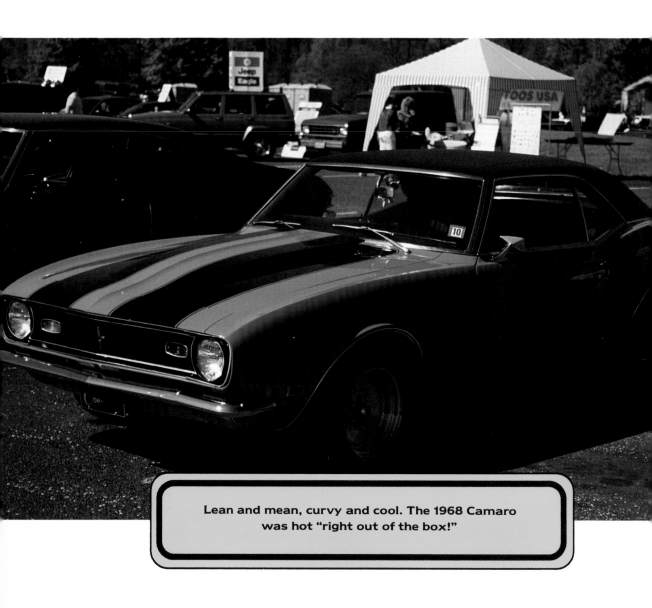

Lean and mean, curvy and cool. The 1968 Camaro
was hot "right out of the box!"

1 THE QUARTER-CENTURY RACE

Tonight, and every night, the grandstand at the drag strip is filled with Ford fans and Chevy lovers. Lately, the Ford fans have had the most to cheer about. Their favorite car, a big blue Mustang, has been shutting down all comers.

*Now Big Blue is about to defend its crown again. The powerful machine rumbles to the line. Heat waves rise from its big **block** engine. Its fat tires bulge like muscles in a bodybuilder's shirt.*

*The driver adjusts his **Nomex** fire-protective mask and tightens his helmet. The he blasts through a perfect burnout to warm the tires…and the crowd. He gets the cheer he's looking for, smiles behind the mask and backs the Mustang to the line for the start. Then he waits.*

He doesn't have to wait long. The Chevy driver roars to the line in a new Camaro. It's as red as fire and looks just as hot!

There's no mistaking the two cars for each other. Mustangs have always had that powerful boxy look, like an army tank ready to roll over anything in its path. Camaros look like cats about to pounce: sleek and curved, low and long. In a moment, though, both cars will be just a blur.

*Now the racers are tensed and ready as the **"Christmas tree"** counts down to the start: Red light…red light…red light…red light…GREEN!*

*In less than a second, four tons of metal become a burst of sound and motion. The Ford surges ahead as the Chevy gets a late start, fumbling for **traction** in a comic dance of spinning wheels and tire smoke. In short order, the Camaro's rubber finds its grip and Chevy Thunder begins to roar. This will be a real race after all!*

Just 12 seconds later, it's over. Who wins this classic Ford vs. Chevy battle? Why, the best car of course!

This Mustang–Camaro race lasted just seconds. But it's part of a longer race between these two speed machines that's been going on for more than 20 years—a race to be the best American **pony car**.

The race began back in the 1960s, a time when babies born after World War II reached car-buying age. The market was full of young car lovers looking for a car to buy. Two of the largest car companies in the world, Ford and General Motors, were locked in a struggle to win the hearts of these young car buyers.

As in the drag race, Ford was the first off the line. They built the Mustang in 1964.

For nearly 2½ years, GM suffered because they didn't have anything like the Mustang to sell. At last, GM introduced its rival to the Mustang. Loud and proud, it was called the *Camaro*. This is the fascinating story of Chevy's affordable dream car and the struggle that turned it from a Mustang copycat into one of the world's great road machines.

 **USA–1**

To understand the Mustang–Camaro battle, you need to know the background of Ford and Chevrolet. It's a little like the history of the Chicago Bears and the Green Bay Packers or the New York Yankees and the Boston Red Sox. In other words, it's a story of neighbors who are bitter rivals.

Back in the early days of the car business, Ford was king. Under Henry Ford, Ford Motor Company invented the modern way of making cars on an assembly line. Henry Ford could build cars faster and cheaper than anyone, and he used these advantages to put America on wheels...Ford wheels.

For a while, nine out of every ten cars sold were Fords. Today, that ratio is one or two out of ten. Almost all of the Fords sold back then were the famous Model T, a simple design built only in the color black. More than 15 million Ts were built in all! By the time the 1920s rolled around, T sales were fading fast. And in many ways, Henry Ford himself created the problem.

As stubborn as he was brilliant, Ford decided that he knew better than the buyers themselves what kind of cars people should have. When his assistants told him that buyers craved larger, more powerful cars than the T, he refused to build then. When other companies added features like the electric starter or better brakes, Henry Ford called them "bunk" and waited for years before adding them. When Ford was told that buyers wanted Model Ts in different colors, he had a ready answer: "They can already have any color they want...*so long as it's black!*"

Not far from Ford's offices was another company that was building cars in many colors...and many sizes and models too. The company had been formed by combining smaller carmakers into one powerful giant. The smaller makers included Cadillac, Buick, Oldsmobile, Oakland (later renamed Pontiac) and Chevrolet. The giant they formed was General Motors.

Chevrolet was the division chosen to battle against the all-powerful Ford. Its cars bore the famous bow-tie emblem and had some powerful weapons. Where the T was powered by a four-cylinder engine, Chevy offered a six at about the same price. The Chevy was larger and more modern-looking than the Ford. And yes, it came in different colors. By the mid-1920s, nothing could stop Chevy's rise and Ford's fall short of a brand-new Ford model...a model Henry Ford refused to build.

When the new Model A Ford finally appeared in 1928, it was too little and too late. Chevrolet had replaced Ford as America's top brand. From that day forward, Chevy has almost always kept that title. That's why, when you see new Chevy models in the company's ads, they often have license plates that read "USA–1."

Ford has never forgotten what Chevy did in the 1920s. Since that time Ford has spent billions of dollars trying to win back the crown. And whenever America's number-two carmaker beats Chevy, there's glee at Ford headquarters.

In Motor City, USA, winning is serious business.

 ## THE CHALLENGE

In the early 1960s, not only was Chevy ahead of Ford, it was beating Ford to a pulp. In the late 1950s, Chevys were among the hottest-selling cars ever built. Fords were less exciting in almost every way.

A smart young executive named Lee Iacocca was rising at Ford with cometlike speed. A master car salesman, Iacocca knew buyers and what they liked. He also knew that the car market was rapidly changing. Millions of young people born after World War II were reaching car-buying age. Iacocca knew these young buyers wanted sporty cars they could afford. If he could get Ford to build a low-priced sportster, he'd have a major hit and a chance to put Ford on top.

The problem was that Chevy was way ahead in sporty cars. Back in 1953, Chevy had built America's first real sports car, the Corvette. The Vette was expensive to buy and a puny seller compared to other Chevies. For each Corvette it rolled onto the streets, Chevrolet sold 40 to 50 of its popular sedans. But the racy

Corvette was Chevy's first sports car, but its high price kept sales down.

1968
RVETTE
DSTER
LLOW
O
RA-MATIC 400
REAR
NO
SS
NDOWS
R ALARM
JoAnn Freund

roadster was a sign of what Chevy and GM could produce.

Chevy also had another sporty car that was more affordable than the Vette, even though the car had never been planned that way. This was a rear-engine car called the Corvair.

The Corvair was meant to be an economy model, but it turned out to be a poor seller. Economy-car buyers were not interested in this "way-out" design with the engine where the trunk usually was. As a last-ditch attempt to save the Corvair, Chevy executives decided to try to sell it to sports-car lovers. They added bucket seats, a floor shift and a racy Italian name: Monza.

Everyone was surprised at the buyers' reaction. The Monza **9** quickly became the hottest-selling Corvair model! Between the Monza and the Vette, the Chevy dealer was the place to go for excitement on wheels.

Back at Ford, Iacocca was having a hard time convincing his company to match Chevy in sports cars. Ford had recently tried to build a new mid-sized car to compete with GM's Pontiac and Oldsmobile lines. The car was a disaster in every way, from its odd name, Edsel, which was the name of Henry Ford's son, to its odd design.

The company was in no mood to try *anything* new. Even so, Iacocca persisted. He begged, borrowed and stole parts from other Ford cars. He bothered his bosses about his sports-car idea every chance he got. Finally he got the go-ahead to try.

Iacocca and his talented team went to work, and the rest is auto history. In April 1964 the car they created, the Mustang, hit the market at full gallop and never slowed down.

It seemed that *everyone* wanted a Mustang. Crowds formed wherever one was parked. People rioted to buy the few available in the first weeks. One man even slept in his new car right in the showroom to make sure that someone else didn't buy it. The newspapers had a name for all this: Mustang mania.

Iacocca and the team at Ford were overjoyed at how well their car was doing. They were also pleased because archrival Chevrolet had nothing with which to fight back. At last, Ford was king again!

With the Mustang, Ford had caught giant General Motors asleep. While the giant sleeps you can get away with a lot. But you have to deal with him when he wakes up. And Ford knew that GM *would* wake up. When it happened, there would be serious danger

10   of getting trampled!

Mustang...the original ponycar! Ford's design was squarish compared with the rounded Camaro.

 ## IF NOT FIRST, BEST!

Long before Ford unveiled the Mustang, there were car builders at GM who favored small, sporty cars. But there were even more engineers, designers and executives who thought the company should spend its time and money on the big, luxury cruisers that GM was famous for. It was this group that got its way. Big cars meant big profits!

But the sports-car fans quietly kept working on their favorite ideas, sketching designs and making models—just in case they were ever needed. That was lucky. When Mustang mania hit, Chevrolet had some ideas on file.

At first, GM didn't think they'd need a sports car. Every large car company has a special department to "spy" on the competition, so GM knew a lot about the Mustang before it ever came out. The verdict: no threat. Compared to the Vette or even the Monza, GM experts felt the Mustang was a pretty meager car. After all, it was built with borrowed sedan parts on a nickel-and-dime budget.

As soon as a Stang was available, GM had it delivered to the company design center. "I looked at it and said it would never sell," recalls Bob Lund, who later became one of GM's most important leaders. "It seemed too boxy and square. It was unappealing."

Sales reports seemed to bear this out. GM executives had sources that gave them information on how well other companies were doing. Forget the news stories, said these sources. Mustang sales are pretty low.

Of course, the sources were totally wrong. Still, GM must have wanted to believe them because month after month went by and GM didn't take any action to meet the threat.

Then in August 1964, Mustang sales passed 100,000 and panic finally hit! Chevrolet knew that each of those 100,000 Mustangs could have been a Chevy. The giant had awoken to discover it had a massive headache.

Suddenly memos started flying down from the 14th floor of the GM building, where the top executives worked. Different parts of the company got the message in different ways, but the meaning was the same: *Do whatever it takes to beat Mustang… and start doing it now!*

There were rules, of course. The new car had to be ready in just over two years, half the time it usually takes. It also had to be made from existing sedan parts, especially parts from an economy car called the Chevy Nova. And perhaps most important, the car had to *beat the Mustang in every way…from roominess to style, power, performance and price.* If we didn't do it first, GM seemed to say, we'll do it best! The new 1967…whatever we call it…is going to be the top-selling sporty car in the whole world!

There were some basic decisions to make. Since the new car would use many parts from the Nova sedan, certain measurements had to be the same. This was a problem because the Nova was high and boxy, while the designers wanted the new sportster low and sleek. Also, because the idea was directly copied from Ford, the new car had to have a completely different look.

Fortunately, the company had such a look: rounded yet muscular. You could see it in the Corvette and the latest version of the Monza. Some called it "swoopy."

But the new car had to be extra special inside and out. GM designers borrowed ideas from jet aircraft for its body design. Scientists had found that if a jet's body were pinched narrow in the center, like a Coca-Cola bottle, airflow improved. The new car similarly got a "Coke-bottle" waistline.

Jets also had a flat black panel that wrapped around the nose to keep reflected sunlight from bouncing off the plane's metal "skin" into the pilot's eyes. The new car got a black stripe around its nose, though the look was closer to that of a bumblebee than a jet plane.

The designers first drew up their ideas. Then clay models were built, painted and trimmed like real cars. The shape was exciting—and different from the new Ford. Fenders had humped tops suggesting the muscles of a sleek jungle cat. And while the Mustang's roof was squarish, the Chevy's roof swept back in a streamlined curve from the windshield to the small, sporty trunk.

The most noticeable part of any car is its front end, or "face." On the Mustang, this was a high, boxy scoop, with the car's horse emblem in the center. In contrast, the grille on the Chevy was a

Like the Mustang, the Camaro was built from sedan parts. But you'd never know it from this wildly customized '67.

The SS, or Super Sport, was the hottest Camaro in the late 1960s. To get hideaway headlights, though, you needed the RS, Rally Sport, package.

simple oval, with the famous blue bow-tie front and center. Almost every line was rounded to contrast with Ford's square look. There was no mistaking the differences between the two rival cars.

As designers worked almost around the clock on the outside of the new car, other specialists were shaping the **interior.** Here the ideas came from Chevy's own Corvette.

A new Vette had been planned for 1968. As part of the plan, designers had created a fantastic new dashboard with deep, sunken dials. Designers now grabbed this whole look. Buyers would get the Corvette dash in the sporty car a full year before the Vette was out! And for thousands of dollars less!

While the designers sketched, the engineers were busy with their slide rules and computers. A major decision was made about the engines. Like the Mustang, the Chevy would offer a range of engines from mild to wild.

The old Chevy six cylinder was mild. It could just wheeze its way to 140 horsepower through a single-barrel carburetor. The next step up was a 155 horsepower six. After that the engines were powerful V-8s.

One V-8 was Chevy's classic "small block," offered in either 302- or 327-cubic-inch sizes, with horsepower up to 275. Any one of the eights was a rocket compared with the six. The extra two cylinders changed the car from a mild-mannered "secretary special" to a real performer.

For those who wanted the ultimate, there was Chevy's "big

"Chevy's fast friend" was even faster when this 327-cubic-inch "small block" V-8 was under the hood.

block" V-8. This was a fire-breathing 396-cubic-inch monster pumping up to 375 horsepower. It was serious machinery, for top drivers only!

The buyer's choice also extended to transmissions. The standard unit was an ancient three-speed manual, with a gearshift on the steering wheel. This was a very unsportscarlike arrangement. A sports car usually had a floor shift in either three or four speeds. There was, of course, an automatic, which also worked on a floor shift. Buyers could also choose power-assisted steering, brakes and windows, air conditioning, cruise control, extra instruments and much more. The car could be as plain or fancy, as low buck or high dollar as the buyer wanted to make it.

If you looked underneath the new car, you'd see that the engineers had chosen to build it in an unusual way. Most cars of the time had a long, ladderlike frame where the engine and other key parts were mounted. The body fit over this like a clamshell.

The frame gave the car its strength. Once the wheels and running parts were bolted on, you could actually drive the frame without the body.

Other carmakers used a **unibody** in which the body itself *was* the frame, with no separate frame underneath. This was a more advanced system, but it was also more expensive.

The new Chevy had a **stub frame**—sort of half frame and half unibody. It was lighter than the ladderlike frame or the unibody, and cost less to build. But some engineers were concerned that it was not as solid a design.

The rear end of the new pony car was also unusual. Most cars at the time, had **leaf springs** at the rear, like those on a wagon or baby carriage. Long strips of metal were bunched together like a bundle of straws. Then the rear axle was hung from the bunches. It was the bunching that gave the springs strength.

In contrast, the new Chevy hung its rear axle from a single strip of metal, a spring design called **single leaf.** Again, some engineers were concerned that this might not be the best design to keep the rear wheels under control. The spring might flex and bend, especially when the car was making tricky turns or driving on bumpy roads. The rear wheels could lose their solid, flat-footed contact with the road.

These designs were completely safe under normal driving conditions. And they did keep the cost down. But the new car was supposed to be a performance car. And some engineers thought there were better ways to build it.

By December 1964 the Mustang was closing in on an astounding 400,000 sales and had already earned Ford more than a billion dollars. It was the most successful new car in nearly 60 years of building Fords!

GM executives watched Ford's success in frustration. But they also slept a little easier knowing that the basic design of their Mustang-fighter was locked in place. Now it was time to start adding finishing touches and working out model types. The car would roll out in two body styles, a sharp coupe and a sleek convertible. And buyers could add on two special "packages." These were the "RS" and "SS" equipment groups.

"RS" stood for "Rally Sport" and was more show than go. It included such head-turning options as hidden headlights, a fancier interior and the bumblebee nose stripe.

The "SS" came from "Super Sport" and was the "go" option. It featured a powerful V-8 and performance chassis.

If you wanted to spend some money, you could buy both options: an "SS" with "RS" trim. Then you'd have both show and go on the same car. Who could ask for more? But the car still lacked one major finishing touch—its name.

The original Camaro got a beefier look in 1969. This one has both the SS and RS packages.

5 INTRODUCING THE...CAMAOR??!!

Whenever a new car is built, the naming process often causes big problems. Everybody has his or her own idea about what the car should be called. And sometimes the naming process can have some weird results.

Chevrolet uses letter codes for its car bodies (the Corvette is the

"Y-body"), so the new sportster was first dubbed the "F-car."

Designers, though, needed something more exciting than "F" to work with. So drawings started showing up with the name "Panther" stenciled on the car's sleek nose. Others pushed for "Wildcat," a name used on several Buick dream cars.

These names were exciting, but GM executives were officially against racing and didn't want any name that went too far in that direction. So when the time came for setting an official name, Panther and Wildcat were out of the question. So was anything else suggesting speed or animal fury.

There were lots of other choices. GM looked at more than 5,000 names before making a final selection. For a while, the car was called GM-Mini. This became Gemini. But nobody really wanted that name to stick.

Anything starting with the letter "C" had an edge. Almost all newer Chevrolet models had "C" names like Corvette, Chevelle; Chevy II and Corvair. Executives liked how they sounded after "Chevy." So that's where the search led. But it led to dead end after dead end. And time was running out. The factories were almost ready to roll. Desperation set in!

Then came the answer. Former Chevy manager Bob Lund tells the story: "One morning [GM vice-president] Ed Rollert and I got together and we went over all the names. We had English–French and Spanish–English dictionaries. Finally I found this word *camaro*, which had a kind of a ring, a dramatic sound, and I said, 'Here's a heck of a name!'"

Lund and Rollert checked the dictionaries for what the name meant. "One definition was 'friend' or 'warm friend,' something like that," recalls Lund. "Perfect for the car."

But there were also other definitions that were not so perfect. One meaning for *camaro* was "a shrimplike creature with many legs found in salt or fresh water." Even worse, another, similar-sounding word meant something like "sick to your stomach." GM executives would have felt pretty sick if that meaning ever got connected to their car.

In the end, GM executives went with the name. Chevy Camaro sounded great. And that was that.

There were other developments. Word had gotten to GM that when the Camaro finally got to the showrooms, it would have a lot more competition than just the Mustang. Ford was building a fancier version of the Mustang, called the Cougar, to be sold through its Lincoln–Mercury dealers. The Chrysler Corporation was pouring money into a model called the Plymouth Barracuda. That led to the worst cut of all. Chevy's sister division, Pontiac, began asking for their own sporty car. In time, they were told to do their own version of the F-car instead. It was called the Firebird. Now the Camaro would have even more competition—from its own company! But top executives did decide that Pontiac would have to wait until several months after the Camaro was introduced before the new Pontiac could hit the showrooms.

Introduction day, September 12, 1966, arrived a little over two years after the planning began. The new Camaro was finally ready to take on the world.

The introduction of any new car is an exciting time. The Camaro's was twice as exciting…since it had two introductions!

First came the introduction of the name. Reporters had discovered that designers were calling the unfinished car "Panther," and they were filing stories about the new beast under that name. That had to be stopped.

Chevy managers called a news conference. Then as cameras clicked, six college women in cheerleader outfits bounded into the room. Each woman carried a letter in the name C-A-M-A-R-O.

They lined up on a stage. Unfortunately, one woman was out of place. So the first official look America got at the name was C-A-M-A-O-R. *What's a Camaor?* reporters wondered.

The news conference worked...sort of. Reporters stopped calling the car by the wrong name. Instead they used the right name...and spelled it wrong, usually "Camero." That still happens today, some 25 years later.

The car's introduction was more successful. Showing off a hot-looking SS convertible at the GM proving grounds, Chevy manager Pete Estes set his first-year sales goal at 300,000. Then reporters got press releases chock full of all the advantages Camaro had over Mustang. And they learned that the new Chevy would sell at a slightly lower price than its Ford rival. "This could be the most exciting sales race in years," one reporter later wrote.

Several reporters got to test-drive the Camaro. Some writers noted that the single-leaf **suspension** wasn't up to the task of controling the rear wheels, just as the engineers had predicted. Hard driving could set up a mean **wheel hop.** But most of the reporters were pleased. "It's a handsome-looking buzzard," wrote Tom McCahill, a top writer of the time. He noted that zero to 60 came and went in eight seconds and that the car had 118 mph top speed. "Should give Ford a heck of a run for the money," wrote another.

Sensing a cat fight, reporters quickly flocked to Ford to see what they thought of Chevy's new Mustang-fighter. The official answer was cool and businesslike. "They're adding buyers to the sporty-car market," said a top Ford manager, "not taking ours away. We're the leader in sporty cars, and we're going to be the leader in every kind of car, probably this year!"

Privately, Ford managers had other things to say. One called it the "Parrot" for its perfect imitation of Ford's idea. Others had

23

Mustang vs. Camaro. Which is better? Fans have argued over this for more than 25 years!

found the shrimp definition of Camaro and pointed it out. Luckily, it wasn't the sick-to-your-stomach definition instead!

Reporters rushed back to Chevy and waited for the counter-punch. "Yes, a Camaro is a kind of animal," smiled a bow-tied division spokesman. "It's the kind that eats Mustangs."

The only reactions that really counted were those of the buyers. And the Camaro got off to a fast start. Not fast enough to catch Ford, though. For each Camaro sold, Ford sold two Mustangs. *How in the world can we catch up with a two-year head start?* Chevy managers wondered.

THE MARK OF "Z"

There *was* a way to catch up. Car companies have long known that racing successes make sales successes. If it wins on Sunday, the saying goes, it will sell on Monday. This is especially true for the sports-car market.

Unfortunately for Chevy, Ford had a head start there too. Since the early 1960s Ford had been running a powerful racing program. GM, on the other hand, wouldn't even allow fast-sounding car names!

Chevy managers decided to try to sneak something through. One popular racing event of the time was the Trans-Am Series, a string of road races for cars the size of the Mustang. Ford was already actively competing, often with the help of a race-car builder from California named Caroll Shelby.

Chevy quietly asked its engineers about preparing a special-model Camaro for Trans-Am racing. And in November 1966, a very different kind of Camaro suddenly appeared at a Trans-Am race in Riverside, California. It featured a superhot 302-cubic-inch version of the small block V-8. This powerplant would make for very fast motoring, so special speed parts were built in all over the suspension system.

The raciest of all Camaros had no special name. In this case, the letter code happened to be Z–28. That code would become famous in the years that followed.

Of course, Chevy made it clear that this new superfast Camaro was *not* for racing. That would have been against GM rules! Instead, it was only for Camaro drivers seeking top performance for their road cars.

Naturally, private racing teams who didn't have to follow GM

How do you spell ultimate Camaro? "Z-28!"

rules ignored that and rushed to order Z-28s for the track.

As 1967 began, Camaro Z-28s were beginning to run at major races. And slowly but surely, even top GM management started to show some interest. They allowed Chevy to place a Camaro as the pace car for the 1967 Indy 500. And when asked if this went against GM's antiracing policy, the company's president surprisingly said, "I see no harm in it."

Chevy engineers probably jumped for joy! Of course the

president's boss, the chairman of the board, went on to say that racing was not necessary. But everyone knew that there would be no putting the cork back in the bottle once it was out. GM cars were being raced, with factory help, like it or not!

When the last 1967 Trans-Am race had been run, Mustang had won the series. But Camaro had taken three races, including the last two, and had done well in the others. The Z had left its mark all over the track.

Sales charts had marks from the Z too. The 1967 Mustang had never been seriously challenged by Camaro. With its 2¹/₂ year head start, Ford's fast pony racked up some 443,000 sales, against 201,000 for Chevy's little "friend." But things were moving in the right direction and Chevy was pleased. Especially since they knew something really special was already on the drawing boards.

 # 7 EVERYMAN'S FERRARI

When the first Camaro took to the roads in late 1966, the *next* Camaro was already being planned. Chevy's mission was simple: establish the Camaro as the nation's number-one sporty car, and finish Mustang off once and for all! Giant GM was fully awake now and ready to throw its weight around!

This wouldn't happen in 1968 or 1969. Those years were set aside for minor improvements to the original design. Then 1970 would be Camaro's year. There would be no panicky rush, no halfway answers. It would be the *year they did everything right.*

Planning began in the design studios. "We said that this second Camaro had to be the ultimate, a baby Corvette," said Chevy manager Pete Estes. "We put our best guys on it, made it lower, worked hard on the styling. We said it had to be the most beautiful automobile we had ever designed."

The top GM designer in those years was William L. Mitchell. Mitchell had been designing cars at GM since the 1930s. He was determined to deliver an absolute knockout of a new Camaro. But to do it, he'd have to fight off the things that "uglify" almost all car designs.

Mitchell knew that every design starts out beautiful. His talented crew couldn't draw an ugly car, even if they wanted to. But once the drawings were done, the changes began. The engineers came first, telling designers there was no room for a man with a hat under that low roof, nor room for an air filter under that swoopy hood. Changes were made.

Then came the money counters. "Sure those fat tires look powerful," they might say, "but we have a special price with the tire company for the thinner, smaller size so you'll have to use them." More changes were added.

Last would come the factory experts. "The curves you've put into that window glass are gorgeous," one might say, "but our glass-forming machines can't handle them. Straighten them up." Even more changes had to be made.

And throughout the process, top executives who just didn't like something would demand still more changes. By the time an inch had been added here and there, and a curve or line changed even a little, a beautiful car would become taller, fatter and dumpier. That's one reason designers love doing "dream cars." It's the one chance they get to create exactly what they want.

Bill Mitchell decided to try to protect the Camaro team from having their work gobbled up this way. He put the project in a special room and allowed no one except team members and a few key executives inside. And he had the designers work fast so that the new car would be well under way before word about the project got around.

There was one group that had to be involved in Chevrolet's secret. Pontiac had introduced the Firebird, its own version of the F-car. The new 1970 Firebird was to use many Camaro parts, so the two design groups had to cooperate. This was not a problem, though. Pontiac's motto at GM is "We Build Excitement!" And its designers are great sports-car lovers like those at Chevy.

To keep the two cars from looking the same, Pontiac and Chevy designers were not usually allowed to see each other's creations. Design-center bosses carried messages between the studios.

Mitchell's directions were to go wild, but keep it smooth. His inspirations were the Corvette and the Ferrari. He told his people to stay away from chrome, scoops and other design tricks. The shape of the body had to say it all!

One problem designers had involved the roofline. The designers wanted it tight and short, on top of a long, sleek body—like the cockpit of a jet fighter. But the Camaro was a four-seat car. It needed a rear-seat window that passengers could see through, but it was messing up the design.

All kinds of different shapes were tried. Then somebody had a brainstorm: Leave the back window off. Instead, make a long front window that rear-seat passengers could see through. This made the look completely different and much smoother. It also saved money on parts, making the car cost less.

The interior experts were busy trying to keep up with the performance lovers next door who were working on the outside. From the beginning, they wanted a "cockpit" look, with instruments wrapped around the driver in a special pod. The problem was that this look would be expensive. Nevertheless, the interior

Sharp wheel rims can turn a car's looks from mild to wild!

designers stuck to their guns. As a result, the interior of the second-model Camaro is one of its most beautiful and unusual features.

Finally, in late 1968, a final model sat in the design-center display room. Mitchell called in the design team. "Are you guys happy?" he asked. "Yes sir!" came the shouted reply. "Okay, then. Don't let anybody screw it up!" Everyone knew that the engineers and money counters were about to land on their new car like vultures.

As always, it was an enormous battle. Some engineers insisted there was no way to get all the necessary engine parts under the car's low hood. Others attacked from the underside, insisting the car had to sit higher off the road to clear the **muffler** and suspension. And one person demanded that huge chrome bolts be driven into the car's smoothly shaped bumpers.

For once the designers had a friend in the engineering department. He was Alex Mair, recently made director of engineering. Mair was a sports-car lover himself, and he pushed to save the beautiful design. New engine and underpan parts were created, even though they cost more. But the convertible model was dropped, which saved some money. This second-model Camaro was sold only as a hardtop—though add-on sunroofs and T-tops came later.

When all was said and done, both the designers and the engineers were proud of what they'd created. But neither group was sure how the sporty-car lovers of the world would react.

Then came the day superstar racing driver Stirling Moss visited GM. Mitchell hauled the new Camaro into the display room. Then he brought Moss in to see it.

"You're going to sell this as a Chevrolet?" Moss gasped. "*A production model?*" Mitchell could see the car had completely floored one of the world's racing greats. Moss could not believe this beautiful dream car could be had by anyone for a few thousand dollars at any Chevy dealer. But that's just what was about to happen.

 ## RUNNING OUT OF GAS

The new Camaro was due on the street in September 1969, along with other 1970 Chevy models. But last-minute problems caused by the changed design made that impossible. Chevy decided to sell 1969 cars as 1970 models until the new car was ready. Then it would be introduced as a 1970$^1/_2$ model.

That day didn't come until early the following year. Chevy

managers rolled out the new car on February 13—Friday the 13th.

The date brought good luck. The new car was a hit from the first glance, especially with car magazines. "The new Firebird and Camaro are the first of a new kind of American GT car," wrote *Car and Driver*. "They're low and sleek, a blend of comfort, handling and silence beyond anything the world has seen at this price!" Others agreed.

Only snooty, foreign-car loving *Road & Track* had a problem with the design. "Too much like older-model Ferraris and Maseratis," sniffed the editors. Some problem—looking too much like a Ferrari!

As before, the new Camaro had a wide choice of engines and transmissions. They ranged from a 155 horsepower six cylinder to both small block and big block V-8s of up to 375 horsepower. The old stub frame was still around, but improvements had made it stronger. And single-leaf rear springs had been replaced by a multileaf design. Added to the new lower and wider stance, the leaves helped the car ride more smoothly and take turns better than the old model. Most of the handling problems were solved. Meanwhile, the Mustang had gotten fatter and duller with time. That made Camaro the best car in the sporty-car market! The mission was accomplished!

Unfortunately, the car market was not what it had been in the recent past. The youth boom that allowed for the sale of more than half a million sporty cars in a year had tailed off. At the same time, more and more makers had jumped into the race. There was also added competition from foreign companies like Toyota and Nissan.

There was also a major factory strike at GM plants, shutting them down for weeks. All these things made sales drop to only 148,000—53,000 *less* than the old body had sold in its first year.

What a disappointment!

The second-generation Camaro was born in the mid-1970s. One writer said that it looked "too much like a Ferrari!"

But Camaro's disappointments were only beginning. In fact, the designers would never have imagined it, but their beautiful new Camaro would soon be in danger of being choked by **air pollution,** strangled with seat belts and starved by a lack of gasoline!

For sports-car lovers everywhere, the 1970s would be a decade of nightmares!

The troubles really began in the mid-1960s. Each year, an incredible number of drivers were losing their lives in car accidents—more than had died in some wars. Citizens and groups across the nation began urging the government to force carmakers to "think safety." This meant the addition of seat belts, better bumpers and other devices, no matter what the extra cost.

About the same time, scientists began to study the quality of America's air and to report serious problems. In some cities, the air was unhealthy to breathe. Auto-exhaust fumes were causing most of the problems. The answer was similar to the one for safety: Use government force to get carmakers to clean up their act. Engine designs had to change and change right away. New exhaust systems had to be invented. Pollution had to be reduced even if performance suffered and prices climbed.

Then came the last straw. In October 1973 a war broke out in the Middle East. Israel was fighting against its Arab neighbors. The United States supported Israel.

There was one big difference between this war and others. The Arabs decided to stop selling their oil to the United States and other nations.

A few years earlier, this wouldn't have been a problem. But Arab oil was cheap and easy to get. So oil companies bought from them instead of digging for oil in the United States. The companies had even closed down U.S. wells.

With one turn of the valve, the Arabs cut off a huge part of America's vital oil supply, the source of our gasoline. Suddenly oil prices skyrocketed. The 30-cent gallon became the 65-cent gallon. And even worse, in many places there was no gas at any price! Long lines formed at the few stations that had gas to sell. People rioted to fill their tanks.

The government acted. Before this "energy crisis" speed limits were as high as 75 mph on some highways. And one state, Nevada, didn't have a speed limit at all. Now every road in the nation was limited to 55 mph to save gas.

In some cities, drivers could buy only a few gallons of gas and only on certain days. If you had an odd license number, you could buy gas on Mondays, Wednesdays and Fridays. Even-numbered

In the 1970s, musclecars like this 396 SS were hit by gas shortages, safety concerns and high insurance rates.

plates could buy on Tuesdays, Thursdays and Saturdays. Nobody could buy gas on Sundays.

As you can imagine, this was not a world where sporty cars thrived. They couldn't use their speed. They couldn't get the gas their high-powered engines craved. And with so many people suffering, it seemed downright wrong to drive a sporty car—a car like the Camaro.

GM and other carmakers did what they could. Teams of engineers and designers who normally worked on new models and higher performance were switched to projects that focused on saving gas, cutting pollution and improving safety. New models were smaller and conserved fuel. Even the Cadillac was reduced a couple of feet in length and put on a diet. Cadillacs dropped nearly a thousand pounds of road-hugging weight.

As for the Camaro, GM's first thought was to dump it altogether. It was a car from another time. Who needed or wanted it?

Even Ford, which invented the high-performance pony car, had given up on it. In 1974 Ford introduced the Mustang II, a tiny coupe propelled by a four-cylinder engine. It looked like a Mustang, with the same jet-intake grille and wild-horse emblem. But it looked like a Mustang that had shrunk in the rain.

With Ford's change, the Camaro and Mustang weren't even in the same ballpark anymore. Other pony cars such as the Barracuda and the Javelin had long since been taken off the market. Only the Camaro and its sister car, the Firebird, were left to hold the pony car flag high.

A meeting was set to talk about whether to let the Camaro live on. All the top GM executives were there. Any of these men could have killed Camaro with one stroke of his pen. As the discussion started, some executives were saying the decision had already been made. The meeting would just make it official.

The big issue was whether to spend the money to update the car to the latest safety standards required by law. If done in the usual way, this would cost a lot. Most people didn't think it was worth it. They wanted to shut down the project.

A few people in the room felt differently... and they felt strongly. These were the men who'd sweated and labored to build the beautiful new style just three years before. Many were in love with the car and it showed. They were willing to do *anything* to save it.

The top executives listened to both sides. Somehow their hearts were moved, and in the end they agreed to a deal. If the car's defenders could come up with a cheap way to meet the standards, the Camaro could live. Some models, including the Z-28, were discontinued.

"We got to work on it, and we worked on reducing the bill," remembers Bob Dorn, former Camaro chief engineer. "The cost was in the multimillions when we started. When we finished, we had it down to a very low number. All that added together to keep the car going."

Going... but not going strong. For the next several years, the Camaro lived on the back burner at GM. There were changes and improvements, but only those that were needed by law or easily borrowed from other GM projects.

Slowly, Camaro sales improved. The Arabs turned the oil tap on in March 1974, and that helped. Sports-car lovers who were turned off by the little mini-Mustang turned to the Camaro instead. And the young, hot-rodder group that always loved the car stuck by it faithfully. Camaro sales had dropped as low as 70,000. By the mid-1970s, they'd doubled that dismal figure, and the danger of discontinuing was over. The big question was "What next?"

First, in 1977, came a complete freshening. The now-classic body got a sleek new front end, a larger back window and several

In 1977 the Camaro got a wraparound rear window. But the biggest change was yet to come—the new "aero" Camaro.

new models. One very famous canceled model, the Z-28, also came back to life.

The results were amazing. Sales jumped sky-high! Almost a quarter of a million Camaros were sold in 1978, and more than 54,000 of them were Z-28s. The car had never sold so well! Mustang sales that year had also improved...up to 179,000. Could the market actually be coming back to life?

A totally new model had been talked about for years. Designers, weary of working on boring sedans, had played with ideas for a new Camaro. Nobody thought such a car would be approved, but that's exactly what happened. GM decided to take a gamble on the Camaro. A brand-new car was okayed for the early 1980s.

9 A NEW WORLD

Serious work on the third Camaro began as early as 1975. And designers who'd done the second body soon realized that they were working in a whole new world. The second car had been a classic all-American muscle machine. There was never any question that there would be a big, beefy V-8 under the hood, driving the rear wheels. That's the way they'd always built them at USA–1.

But by the mid-1970s everything was changing. GM had already made the decision to go to front-wheel drive on many of its new sedan models. Most engines would be four cylinders, and six cylinders were the maximum. Every car in the line—from the littlest Chevy to the biggest Cadillac—was getting smaller. Even the ocean-liner-sized Cadillac was shrinking!

That meant the new Camaro would be smaller and lighter too. But would this be the first front-wheel drive pony car? And would tomorrow's driver find only a six-pack of power under the gas pedal?

By 1978, though, the company had made a major decision. GM would keep the new car rear-wheel drive. That gave the designers a fresh start and a chance to keep the basic long-hood, short-rear look that had made the second body such a hit. Idea after idea had been tried—maybe 50 different looks in all. Many were spectacular. But none was a *Camaro*.

At the time, the job was in the hands of a team working in the basement of the GM design center. One team member, Roger Hughet, was sketching the day away when suddenly his pencil drew something startlingly different. It was a car with a long glass rear roof—a single sheet of stream-lined glass that flowed from the backseat right to the tail. Lots of sketches showed glass roofs, but this one was somehow different.

Hughet looked at what he'd done and raced to show it to his boss, Bill Porter. Porter took a look and raced upstairs to the office of Irv Rybicki, who ran the entire operation. Rybicki had taken over when Bill Mitchell retired.

"We took one look at Roger's drawing," recalls Rybicki, "and that was all I needed. I said do it full size, and it was a success from the very beginning."

The design was then made into a clay model and moved outside to a special viewing yard. A 1978 model was moved outdoors and parked next to the new model. Hughet, Porter, Rybicki and others walked around and around both cars, viewing them from all angles. "Suddenly the current car looked dated," says Rybicki. The design team knew they had it! From that point on, it was just a question of working out the details.

The roof was what made the new Camaro design special. No production car has ever had a roof like it. It's one of the largest pieces of glass ever put on a car. It's curved in three directions at once. It's also strong enough to act as the car's trunk. You can slam it down without breaking it.

Glass-company engineers nearly had a fit when they saw what the GM designers wanted them to make. Nobody had ever shaped a piece of glass like that, let alone produced hundreds of thousands of them. But the promise of selling all those new rear windows to GM was enough to keep them trying.

The window makers created sample after sample. Each one of them was expensive. Some were rejected because they were the wrong shape. Others were difficult to see through. The glass was fuzzy. Still more weren't strong enough. "We went through probably 35 samples before we nailed it down," says Rybicki. "But it's there and it's beautiful!"

The rest of the car is pretty impressive too. The lines begin at a front end that's both clean and unusual. It has no grille in the usual sense. Instead, the car is what's called a **bottom feeder,** taking in engine air under the bumper.

Headlights are sunken into the shape and have their own story. Both Camaro and Firebird designers wanted four-headlight units and both wanted them to pop in and out of the bodywork. GM executives felt this was too expensive and told the designers to choose either two hidden lights or four that could be seen. Pontiac took the two, Chevy the four.

One thing you can't tell is how much smaller the new car is. It's a full ten inches shorter than the second body, and two inches narrower. Weight is reduced by about 500 pounds! With less weight to lug, the car is both faster and more economical.

The car is also lighter, more comfortable and airier inside. The trunk is bigger too. The new Camaro just flat out *works* better than any Camaro in history, and it looks better.

Climb aboard and you'll see more improvements. The interior design team began with the idea of making the dash like one in a private jet. Aircraft have the same kind of deeply shaded instrument panel. The aircraft look continues in the windshield, one of the most streamlined ever on an American car. The glass comes right up to your eyes, so you never feel as if you're looking out of a long tunnel. Instead, your **line of vision** is right out on the road.

One strange thing about this new Camaro is the glove box. There isn't any! Modern cars are run with lots of little computers. These minibrains can't stand the heat under the hood so they're installed in the instrument panel. There's no room for a glove box! **41**

The third-generation Camaro shows how much fun can be packed into an affordable package. Here's a 1986 IROC-Z model.

As did the designers, the engineers had to work on a front-wheel drive model. Then they switched back to rear-wheel drive. The biggest change they made was to the famous stub frame. After 15 years of living with it, they finally got rid of it. The Camaro became a true unibody car.

The new body was also an excuse to change the car's suspension. The front end received **struts,** which save both weight and cost over the old **A-arm** system. The rear end got rid of the bunched leaf springs that had ousted the old single leaf. Instead, the rear now had softer-riding **coil springs,** with extra parts to keep everything under control. The new car rode better and handled better.

In the engine room the classic small block V-8 still ruled. But those wanting better economy could have either a four-cylinder engine or a V-6. These smaller engines could handle the lighter car without bogging it down. Few owners chose the four, but the V-6 was popular.

All design work was completed by late 1978, in time to sell the car as a 1982 model. Before introduction day, Irv Rybicki and other top GM executives took a fleet of the new F-cars on a final test run. "We were out in Arizona," says Rybicki, "when a group of people in sports cars started chasing us. When we stopped, they asked what our cars were, since there were no nameplates on them. Of course, we couldn't tell them anything. But one fellow said that whoever built them, they were better-looking than any Ferrari."

 A CAMARO FOR TOMORROW

The third Camaro is soon coming up on its tenth birthday. Changes over the years have been few, yet the design still looks as good as the day it was born in 1982. What will tomorrow's Camaro be like?

Like Irv Rybicki, GM will never tell. But there have been hints. For some time, GM has been at work on a secret sporty car called the GM-80. It has a plastic skin like a Corvette, but front-wheel drive. It's said to have a V-6 engine, probably with a turbo for extra power. The best bet is that this car, or something like it, will be the basis for the next Camaro and Firebird, due in the mid-1990s.

People who've seen the GM-80 say that it looks a lot like the

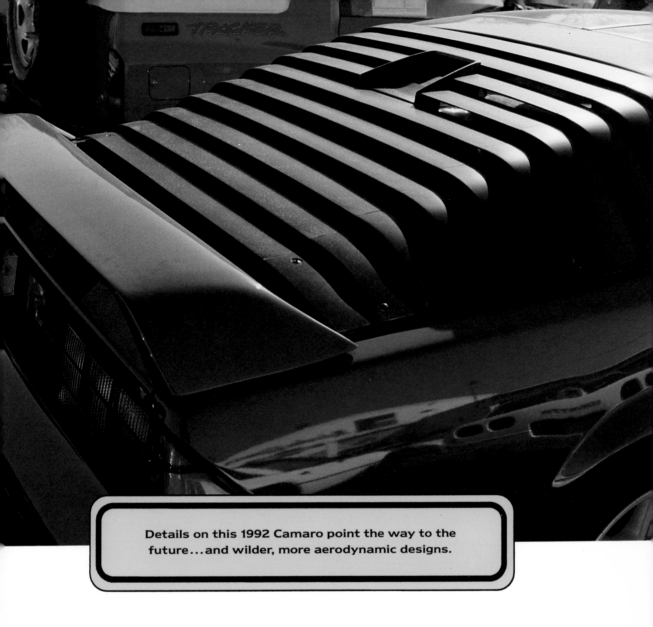

Details on this 1992 Camaro point the way to the
future...and wilder, more aerodynamic designs.

current third-body Camaro but is smaller and sleeker. And it's got
the big rear-glass window.

Beyond that, it's anybody's guess. Like other cars of the future,
the new Camaro will get more and more electronic and high tech.

Engines will probably get smaller and use less gas, without
losing power. GM has experimented with **two-cycle engines**, like
those in a lawn mower but much more efficient. A two-cycle engine

makes power twice with every turn of the engine, compared to making it once each turn in the four-cycle engines now used in cars. That means the engine can make the same power with less weight. Look for a two-cycle engine in your Camaro of the 21st century.

Tomorrow's Camaro will also be built of new materials. Today's heavy steel will give way to more and more plastic. There will also be lots of **composites,** mixtures of materials that are both strong and light. Many of the composites will be made from carbon, the material that makes coal black. Carbon-based composites are now the way to go in high-performance machines, from Grand Prix racing cars to fighter jets.

Your Camaro will also help the environment. The engine will make very little pollution, but that will be only the beginning. Every part of the car will be recyclable. Take a picture of the next junkyard you see! Within a few years, junkyards may be a dying breed.

Some things will not change. Since its "Panther" days, the Camaro has always been sporty, youthful and affordable. That's going to continue as long as there is a Camaro. And there's a good chance that this Cool Classic from Chevrolet will be around for a long time to come!

# GLOSSARY/INDEX

A-arm 43 An A-shaped metal part holding a wheel to the frame or body. A-arms are mounted on hinges so the wheel can move up and down. They are usually connected to springs to absorb bumps.

air pollution 33, 34, 46 The dirtying of the air with smoke or fumes sent forth from car exhausts, factory smokestacks and other sources.

block 5, 17, 18, 25, 32, 44 The central part of an engine; houses pistons, crankshaft and other major parts.

bottom feeder 41 A car that gets its engine air from below the front bumper rather than through the grille.

"Christmas tree" 5 The starting signal at a drag race; made up of red and green lights mounted on a pole. The reds flash down the pole, followed by the green, starting the race.

coil spring 43 Thick metal bar, bent into a twisting spiral shape and used to absorb shocks from car wheels. When most people think of what a spring looks like, it's a coil spring.

composites 46 Lightweight, strong mixtures of materials used to make auto and aircraft body parts.

interior 16, 19, 29, 30, 41 Inside areas of a car.

leaf springs 18, 32, 43 Long, flat strips of metal used as springs. Usually bundled together for strength, then used to mount the rear axle of a car.

line of vision 41 Measurement designers use to check how much a driver can see through the windshield while seated in the car.

muffler 30 Tubular part placed in an exhaust pipe and used to quiet the exhaust sound of a car.

Nomex 5 Fire-resistant fabric used in driver's protective masks and driving suits.

pony car 6, 18, 36, 39 Small, low-cost, high-performance coupe. So named because the first pony car was the Mustang.

single leaf 19, 23, 32, 43 Leaf spring made of only one flat metal bar instead of the usual bundle.

strut 43 Suspension part holding the wheel to the body.

stub frame 18, 32, 43 System of mounting wheels and engine in a car through a half frame connected to the body.

suspension 23, 25, 30, 43 Parts that attach wheels to a car. Usually made to move so they absorb road bumps.

traction 5 The grip tires get on the ground.

two-cycle engine 45, 46 Engine design that produces *two* pulses of power with each turn of the engine. Four-cycle engines produce *one* pulse per engine turn, so a two-cycle produces more power for the same engine size.

unibody 18, 42 Method of building a car in which the body is strong enough to take the role of a separate frame and hold all the parts together.

wheel hop 23 A handling problem in which the rear wheels of a car hop around uncontrollably.

48